Three Little Pigs

Houses from Straw

Three little pigs left home one day.
They packed their bags and went on their way.
Mother Pig said, "Goodbye, bye, bye!"

Goodbye!

Sssshhh!

But a wolf saw them go and thought,
"Mmm — pork pie!"

The first little pig met a man selling straw.
"This will make a good house, I know it, for sure!"
He paid for the straw and stacked it up high,
but the wolf licked his lips, thinking,
"Mmm — stir fry!"

The second little pig met a man selling wood.
"I'll build my house with this — it looks quite good."
He worked all day and did not stop,
but the wolf licked his lips, thinking,
"Mmm — pork chop!"

The third little pig met a man selling bricks.
"These look strong, much better than sticks."
He built his house, all shiny and new,
but the wolf licked his lips, thinking,
"Mmm — barbecue!"

When the homes were finished by the piggies three,
they went inside to cook their tea.
The wolf was feeling hungry too.
He licked his lips, thinking,
"Mmm — pork stew!"

MMM!

The three pigs ran and fetched a pot.
"Quick!" said Piggy Bricks,
"Let's make it hot!"

As the hungry wolf
jumped down the chimney tower,
he landed in the pot, screaming,
"Oww — sweet and sour!"

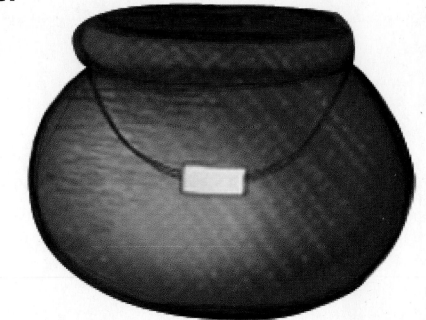

The wolf jumped out and ran far away
from the bricks, the wood and the pile of hay.

The lesson of this story is be careful what you pick.
Think before you act —
make your house out of bricks!

Said the wolf to Piggy Straw, "Now let me in!"
"Not by the hair on my chinny chin chin!"
So the wolf huffed and puffed,
and the house went WHAM!
Then he licked his lips, shouting,
"Mmm — roast ham!"

Piggy Straw ran to the house made of wood.
The wolf said to the pigs, "Let me in! I'll be good!"
The wolf huffed and puffed,
and the house went SMASH!
Then he licked his lips, shouting,
"Mmm — goulash!"

Then the two pigs ran to the house made of bricks.
They were chased by the wolf (who was not quite as quick).
He huffed and he puffed, but the house stayed whole.
So the wolf climbed the roof, shouting,
"Mmm — casserole!"

No Salesmen
No Wolves
Please!

No
Wolves!

An entertaining retelling of the story
of the Three Little Pigs.

Large illustrations and card pages make this
an ideal book to share with a group.

Illustrated by Katie Saunders

Castle Street Press

The Wilderness, Berkhamsted, Hertfordshire, HP4 2AZ.

This edition copyright © 2011 Make Believe Ideas Ltd.
A Ready to Read book. All rights reserved. No part of this publication
may be reproduced, stored in a retrieval system, or transmitted in
any form or by any means, electronic, mechanical, photocopying,
recording, or otherwise without the prior written permission of the
copyright owner.

Printed and bound in Dongguan, China, December 2011.

With thanks to Nick and Claire Page.

Read together

Promotes
enjoyment of
books

0+
YEARS

£6.99

ISBN10: 1-78065-096-5
ISBN13: 978-1-78065-096-8

9 781780 650968